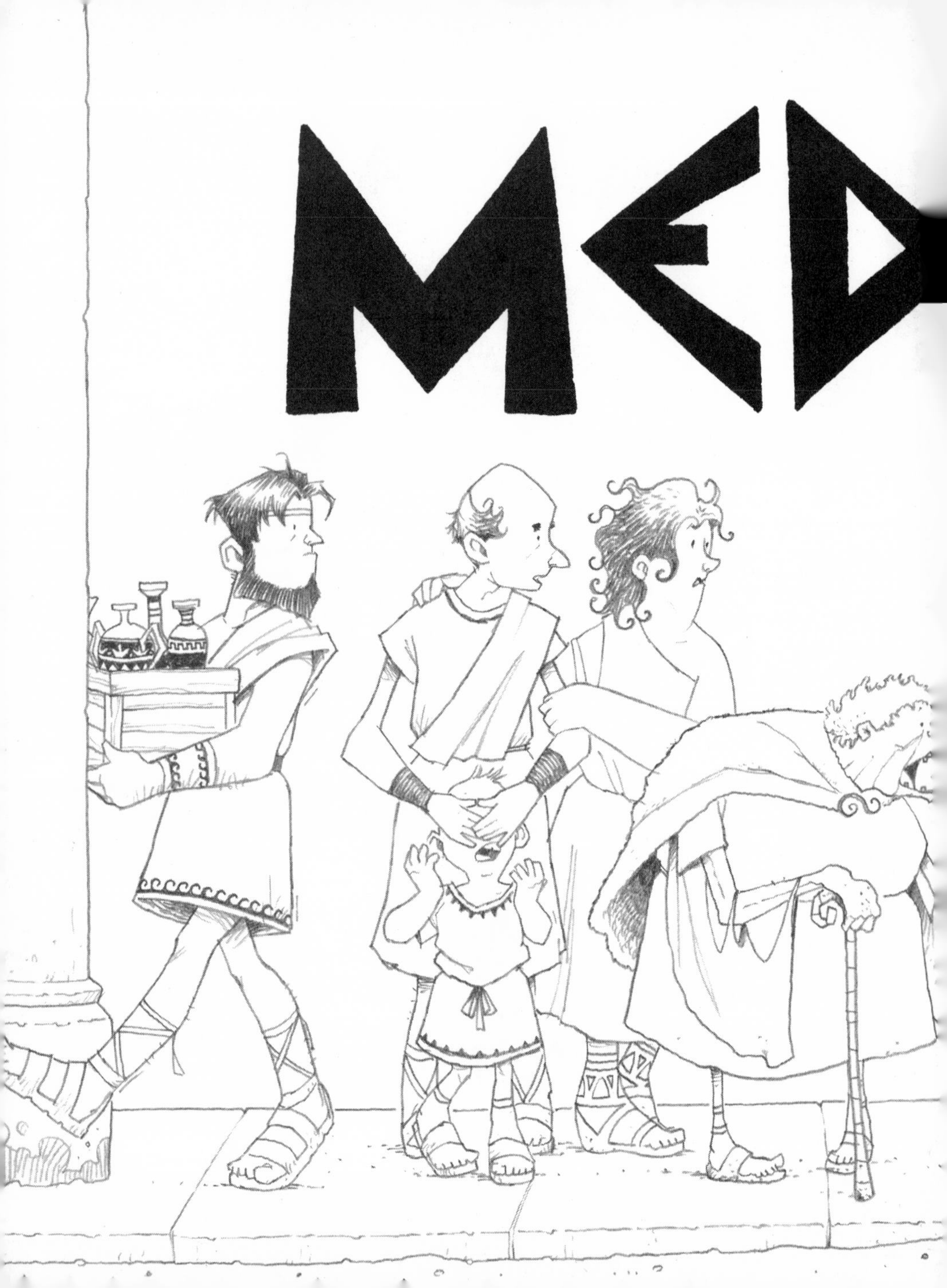
MED

USA
Jones

BY
ROSS COLLINS

ARTHUR A. LEVINE BOOKS
AN IMPRINT OF SCHOLASTIC INC.

Published by Arthur A. Levine Books, an imprint of Scholastic Inc.,
Publishers since 1920. Scholastic and the Lantern Logo are trademarks and/or registered trademarks of Scholastic Inc. · No part of this
publication may be reproduced, stored in a retrieval system, or transmitted
in any form or by any means, electronic, mechanical, photocopying,
recording, or otherwise, without written permission of the publisher.
For information regarding permission, write to Scholastic Inc.,
Attention: Permissions Department, 557 Broadway, New York, NY 10012.

Library of Congress Cataloging-in-Publication Data
Collins, Ross · Medusa Jones / by Ross Collins — 1st ed   p. cm. · Summary:
In ancient Greece, Medusa Jones, a gorgon, and her friends, a minotaur
and a centaur, are mocked and sneered at by the other Acropolis Academy
children whose parents are kings and gods, but when they go on a school
camping trip together, the "freaks" become true heroes · ISBN 0-439-90100-6
[1. Medusa (Greek mythology)—Fiction 2. Mythology, Greek—Fiction
3. Animals, Mythical—Fiction 4. Bullies—Fiction 5. Self-acceptance—
Fiction] I. Title · PZ7 · C6836Me 2008 · [Fic]—dc22 · 2007017199

ISBN-13: 978-0-439-90100-0 · ISBN-10: 0-439-90100-6

10 9 8 7 6 5 4 3 2 1   08 09 10 11 12 13

First Edition, January 2008 · Printed in the U.S.A.

FOR JACQUI —

MY GORGON

A LONG TIME AGO

IN ANCIENT GREECE,

LIVED A LITTLE GIRL NAMED

MEDUSA JONES.

MEDUSA WAS A GORGON.

BUT APART FROM THAT,

PRETTY NORMAL.

CHAPTER 1

"**P**LEEEAASE CAN I TURN THEM TO STONE?" Medusa begged.

"It's not the polite thing to do, dear," said Medusa's mom.

"*They're* not polite," Medusa said. "They were mean about my hair again today."

"Sticks and stones, Medusa," said Medusa's mom. "You can't go turning everyone who's mean about your hair to stone."

"Gran did." Medusa scowled.

"Gran is insane and lives in a cave. Your father and I didn't raise you like that. Anyway, that's not the point, Medusa. You have to work out other ways of dealing with people who get on your nerves."

Medusa sighed and wandered through to the living room, where her dad was hiding behind his paper. She could see a few of his headsnakes curling over the top, trying to read the sports on the back page.

Medusa walked over to his side.

"Dad—" she began.

"No," said Dad.

"But you didn't even know what I was going to—" said Medusa as her dad lowered the paper.

"Yes I do, Med," said her dad. "Can you turn the Champions to stone? No. Your mom's right."

"But they're so mean to me."

"I know they are—but you have to rise above it," said her dad; some of his headsnakes stuck their tongues out at Medusa. The paper snapped back up.

Rise above it. That's what Dad always said. Medusa went out into the garden and sat on the bench, half of which was still getting the sunshine. Her headsnakes curled around one another, fighting for the warmest spot.

The garden was filled with statues of postmen and salespeople. Each one had a look of horror on its face. Some were slightly turned as if to start running. The Jones family had amassed these ornaments over the first few years of Medusa's life, while Gran had still been living with them. Eventually they'd had to pick up their mail from the post office in town as nobody would deliver to the Jones house anymore.

One by one, Medusa's dad had dragged the petrified postmen through to the garden and eventually they

stopped being a hidden shame and had become a lovely decorative feature. Ivy curled up legs and arms. Blue and white flowers sprouted from mail sacks and screaming mouths, and small birds made their nests in the postmen's peaked caps. It was really quite pretty.

The statues cast long shadows across the garden

as the sun got lower in the sky, and when it became too cold to sit out anymore, Medusa went up to her room.

Medusa sat on her bed and started back on the book she had been reading for the past two years. Reading wasn't her forte. She was easily distracted by anything, and her headsnakes had a habit of turning the pages back when one of them had missed an important plot point.

Very soon distraction arrived in the form of a cold, wet sensation on her left knee. Then one on her right knee and one on her foot. She looked down and found her puppy, Cerberus, looking up at her, three times.

Cerberus had three heads, which was at once good and bad. It meant that his sense of smell was second to none. One dog nose is excellent, but three can smell a sausage in the next town. Likewise, he benefited from triple hearing, although this tended to be selective. His three gaping jaws never missed when you threw him a ball, but balls never lasted very long. Best of all, he would lick you—or "kiss" you as Medusa called it—three times as much, which was nice if you liked that sort of thing.

On the downside, each head had its own appetite, which made feeding a nightmare and walking past a child with a cookie extremely dangerous. Three heads meant three times the amount of drool. (Medusa's first job when she got home from school was to mop it all up.) Three heads also had three barks, so just when Medusa's parents had finally persuaded the post office that their employees were safe again, Cerberus arrived and it was back to collecting the mail.

Medusa didn't care. She looked down at his little waggy tail and six big eyes (five brown, one blue). Who couldn't love three faces like that? Cerberus jumped up on the bed and "kissed" Medusa until she could

smell only dog spit and her headsnakes were exhausted from nipping him.

"We'll show them—eh, Cerb?" said Medusa, ruffling his ears.

"We'll show them."

CHAPTER 11

"**I**S IT COLD ENOUGH FOR THAT?" ASKED MEDUSA'S mom.

"No," Medusa said, and walked out into the lovely sunny morning, slamming the door behind her.

Medusa walked down the road trying to avoid people's stares. Hadn't anyone seen a girl in a hat before? Perhaps they had, but not many had seen a girl in a hat that was desperately trying to remove itself. Medusa reached up and pulled the hat firmly back down. Her headsnakes hissed.

"Shut up," Medusa hissed back. "I thought you all liked the heat. Be hot, be happy, be quiet."

Her headsnakes squirmed and writhed around. The hat jiggled on top of Medusa's head, as if she were wearing a large serving of woolen Jell-O. Medusa

13

poked it until the headsnakes settled down, then she turned the corner onto Agamemnon Avenue, where Acropolis Academy stood. From well down the avenue she could see the gateposts, and she could also see who was standing there.

The Champions.

The Champions always stood at the school gates in the morning. They got up early each and every day. Brushed their shiny white teeth, which would be just as shiny and bright if they never saw toothpaste. Put on their dazzlingly white chitons and got to school before everyone else. The Champions considered it their duty to remind everyone of their deficiencies first thing in the morning.

Medusa walked down the avenue, listening to the three prodigies pass judgment on each unfortunate who came their way.

"Ever tried playing connect the dots on your face?"

"Is that your breath or has something died in your chiton?"

"Nice bag!"

But the Champions fell silent when they saw who was coming. Medusa was their favorite. And there was something different about her today.

"Well, look who it is," Perseus sneered, his teeth glowing like a highly polished iceberg. "If it isn't Little Miss Hiss herself."

"Miss Hiss!" echoed Theseus. "HUR HUR HUR, nice one, Pers!" Theseus was also a glowing spectacle of boyhood. Perhaps a bit ungainly—oversized muscles have that effect—but still gorgeous.

"I *know* it's a nice one," said Perseus. "I did come up with it myself after all. Did you hear that, Cassy? Cassy? Are you listening?"

Cassandra wasn't listening; she was entranced by the perfection of her ten tiny toes. Cassandra was, like the rest, too beautiful for words (although Medusa could think of some). Cassandra spent most of her time either admiring herself or fretting over what might go wrong. She was gorgeous but pessimistic.

"Cassy!" barked Perseus.

Cassandra looked up. "Huh?" she said, and then saw Medusa. "Oooh! Look who it is. Little Slitherface herself." She thought for a second. "Perhaps we should leave it, Pers; it can turn people to stone, you know."

"Not allowed to." Perseus grinned. "Mommy and Daddy say no, isn't that right, python puss?"

Medusa scowled and walked toward the

gate, but they quickly lurched together to block her way.

"There's something different about her today." Perseus smiled. "What could it be? Let's see, new sandals? Nope—still old and tatty."

"Perhaps a new *parfum*?" Cassandra grinned and sniffed around Medusa's ears. "No, she still smells like a barn."

"Barns don't smell good," chuckled Theseus to himself.

"But wait! How could we have missed it?" Perseus asked. Medusa's hat began to writhe again so she steadied it with her hand.

"My word, Medusa!" Perseus guffawed. "But what lovely new headwear you have."

"My personal attire is none of your affair," glowered Medusa, now having to hold on to her squirming hat with both hands.

"Oh, but it is," said Cassandra. "We're the fashion police in this school."

"Your hat's against the law," grinned Theseus.

"We take our role very seriously," Perseus said. "We can't allow just any old outfit to enter our school, especially one that may be . . . hiding something."

18

"I'm not hiding anything, so leave me alone," Medusa said, and tried in vain to push past again.

"She says she's not hiding anything, Perseus," Theseus said. "Maybe she's just cold."

"Of course she's not cold, you cretin," whispered Perseus. "Remember . . . ? Hiss hiss . . . ? Slither, slither?" He made a slinky motion with his hand.

"Aaahh." Theseus smiled and looked around at Medusa. "You got snakes for hair. HUR HUR HUR!"

Medusa glared at his big stupid handsome face, wondering what harm she could do it, and didn't notice Perseus reaching toward her. He grabbed Medusa's hat and began to pull.

"Get off!" yelled Medusa. "Leave me alone, you big shiny idiot!" She yanked back at the hat,

which was writhing and punching. It was a three-way struggle.

"HAT! HAT! HAT!" chanted the Champions ingeniously.

"HAT! HAT! HAT!"

"HAT! GRANITE! HAT!"

What? thought Medusa as she struggled. She could have sworn she heard—

GRANITE!

There it was again.

Nobody had said it. It had just popped into her head.

No.

She shouldn't.

IGNEOUS!

Mom would kill her.

SEDIMENTARY!

She didn't even know if she could. . . .

"HAT!" shouted Theseus.

Medusa felt her stomach lurch.

"HAT!" shouted Cassandra.

Medusa's legs started to shake.

"HAT!" yelled Perseus.

Medusa closed her eyes tight.

She felt sick.

Her head suddenly felt eerily cold.

She opened her eyes to see . . .

Perseus standing, grinning. Waving the hat around in glee.

The headsnakes hissed and spat at the Champions, straining in vain to detach themselves from Medusa's head.

Medusa snapped out of her moment.

"Give it back, you pond scum," she yelled.

"Get those things under control, Snakehead!" Cassandra yelled back.

"I'm the son of Zeus," snapped Perseus. "Nobody calls me pond scum. Go get your stupid hat, freak." And with that he tossed the hat over Medusa's head. Medusa looked around and watched her hat land with a dull *squelch* in the gutter. The school

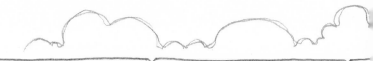

bus slowly pulled onto the side of the road and parked right on top of it. Medusa looked from her hat up to the children on the bus. They were all grinning and laughing, their hands and fingers wriggling behind their heads.

Like snakes.

CHAPTER III

ONCE AND ONLY ONCE EACH YEAR, THERE IS A DAY known as "the longest day." On this day the sun rises earlier and sets later than usual. Today was not that day, but to Medusa Jones it felt as though it was.

The school seemed to have nothing better to talk about all day than Medusa's hat humiliation. Wherever Medusa went, she heard sniggering and whispers behind her. The whispers stopped each time she turned around. Everyone knew about the supposed power of Medusa's gaze, but none were as sure as the Champions that she wouldn't use it at will. The giggling got particularly depressing when she was asked to deliver a note to the staff room and heard the distinct sound of a guffaw from Mr. Achilles, the P.E. teacher, as she left.

It seemed as though the bell would never ring, but eventually it did. After most of the other children had run laughing and shouting to freedom, Medusa packed her satchel and began the walk home. She decided to walk along the main street for a diversion, where she could look in the shop windows and admire the pastries. Medusa and her mother would often go pastry-admiring when in low spirits.

KERAMEIK
POTS

Medusa wandered down the street, ignoring the familiar stares of the townspeople. She paused occasionally to look in the windows, but it seemed that most of the shops had already sold most of their pastries for the day. There wasn't much to see apart from the odd currant bun, which had been squeezed by everyone before they settled on something tastier instead.

After a while Medusa saw a shop she didn't recognize. It was a new shop with a freshly painted front,

gleaming polished fittings, and a large sign hanging outside with a picture of a glamorous lady smiling as though she had just won the lottery. Medusa walked closer and read the words below the blissful woman.

"Fed up with YOU?" read the sign. "A New You is just a snip away!"

Medusa looked up at the sign above the door. In large impressive golden letters, it read:

SALON DE JOSEF
HAIRDRESSING TO THE GENTRY

Medusa wasn't sure what the gentry was, but she liked the sound of it and decided to go in.

The air inside Salon de Josef was thick with perfume and wax. On the walls, there were pictures like the one outside of insanely smiling ladies with outrageous hairstyles. One had a bird's nest atop her head, her hair braided to look like a pelican. Another had her hair styled to resemble a pouncing tiger, but she looked extremely pleased with it. On one side of the room was a row of plush chairs, one of which was occupied by a fat lady with a dog the size of a rat on her lap. The dog yapped at Medusa when it caught sight of her. The fat lady turned to see what the rat was yapping at and immediately stood up and tottered out. Medusa went over and sat where the woman had been; the seat was nice and warm.

On the other side of the room was a row of elevated seats with grand gold-framed mirrors in front of each one. One of them was occupied by a lady who was having her hair transformed into what looked like a monkey on a bicycle. The man who was doing the transforming had his back to Medusa; his arms and hands moved feverishly around the sculpture, a tweak here, a snip there, until finally he stopped dead, threw his tiny scissors on the floor, and shouted *"Voilà!"* He pushed a lever that caused the seat to shoot upward. The woman gazed at her new hair for the first time. The monkey on the bicycle seemed to be laughing and somehow the wheels looked like they were turning.

"Monsieur Josef!" squealed the lady. "I am reborn. YOU are a genius!"

"I know," said Monsieur Josef, and with a flick of his foot, the chair plummeted back to the floor and the woman wobbled out of the salon grinning from ear to ear.

"A moment, Madame Pomfry," said Monsieur Josef with his back to Medusa as he arranged the lotions, combs, and scissors on the shelf below the mirror. He carefully removed all the hair from the chair with a brush the size of a toothpick and finally slapped his hands together and turned around.

Medusa smiled her nicest smile at Monsieur Josef. He was a small pear-shaped man with long elegant fingers and a mustache, which had been styled to curve around his cheeks and into his ears. Monsieur Josef looked at Medusa.

"Hello," said Medusa.

"Oo . . . are you?" said Monsieur Josef. "And wat ave you done weeth Madame Pomfry?"

Medusa had never heard an accent like this before in Greece.

"She left," said Medusa. "I'm Medusa, Medusa Jones." She smiled again.

Monsieur Josef sniffed, but then he caught sight of Medusa's hair. His expression altered to one of interest. "Ave you been ere before?" he asked, and pointed to Medusa's headsnakes. "Eez theez wan of mine?"

"No," said Medusa. "I've not been here before. They're mine."

"*C'est magnifique!*" said Monsieur Josef. "I ave never seen their lak. So real. So . . . snakey."

"Thank you," Medusa said.

"And wat do you want of me?" asked Monsieur Josef, transfixed by the headsnakes.

"I want what the sign says," Medusa answered. "A new me, please."

"But zees ees an original," said Monsieur Josef. "Why would you change zees?"

"I'm sick of being an original," said Medusa. "I want something normal."

"Like wat?" Monsieur Josef asked.

"I don't know," said Medusa. "Just give me the works."

"Ah! Ze warks you weel ave, mademoiselle!"
Monsieur Josef smiled and patted the styling chair.
"Op up eer and Monsieur Josef will . . . create!"

Medusa hopped up onto the seat and a clean
white sheet immediately billowed around her
shoulders and was gently secured at the back of
her neck.

Monsieur Josef then picked up a selection of tiny bottles and began to spray delicate mists across the headsnakes. The first was warm water, the second a light perfume with the scent of lavender, the third something that smelled like honey and gave Medusa a tingling sensation on her forehead. The headsnakes slowly coiled and basked in the warm aromas. They weren't used to such attention; all Medusa did was dunk them in a bucket of cold water once a week.

"So laflike," gasped Monsieur Josef. "Eet eez a shame, and yet once you ave ze monkey on ze bicycle you weel never go back."

He began to massage the headsnakes with his long nimble fingers and they lightly hissed with pleasure. He stretched them out to their full length, kneading each little bone, and let them flop back down. The headsnakes couldn't believe their luck.

"And now, mon petite Mademoiselle Medusa," said Monsieur Josef with a flourish. "Prepare to be . . . transformed!"

Medusa tightened her grip on the armrests; this was the beginning of the rest of her life. Monsieur Josef held aloft a large silver pair of scissors, the light dancing on their blades and dazzling Medusa. With one deft flick of his wrist, Monsieur Josef took his first snip. Instantaneously every single headsnake stopped basking and turned to face their attacker. Monsieur Josef also stopped, his long-fingered hands hovering above the headsnakes.

"So . . . laflike?" he squeaked as every headsnake rose up and then plunged down, jaws gaping, teeth biting, finger munching.

"AAAAAAAAAGHHHHHHHHHH!"
screamed Monsieur Josef, tumbling backward, bottles
and scissors crashing to the floor.

"AAAAAAAAAGGHHHHHH!**"**
screamed Medusa, woken suddenly from her bright
new future.

"Ma beautifool ands!" screamed Monsieur Josef.
"Ma tools!" He held his hands aloft, but the venom
had worked quickly. Monsieur Josef didn't have hands
anymore; he had huge pulsating red balloons on the
ends of his delicate wrists. They looked
like angry udders. The headsnakes
hissed and snapped, trying to
bite their attacker some
more, but Medusa had
jumped off the seat and was
backing toward the door.

"What have you done?" screamed Monsieur Josef, his accent slipping. "You have angry hair? Hair that attacks? What kind of a freak are you?"

"I'm not a freak," said Medusa, backing away from the udders. "I'm sorry about your hands."

"Sorry?" screamed Monsieur Josef. "You are sorry? Get out! You have ruined me! Get out, I say!" He waved one of the udders angrily at the door.

"The swelling will go down in a month," Medusa called, but Monsieur Josef didn't look like he cared. She grabbed her satchel and ran as fast as she could all the way home.

CHAPTER IV

AT LAST THE WEEKEND ARRIVED, THE BEST PART of school. Medusa pulled herself out of bed at a decently unrespectable hour and wandered into the bathroom. She looked at herself blearily in the mirror; the headsnakes all stared back at her resentfully.

Medusa walked slowly downstairs, listening for the familiar sound of little running paws skittering through the house. Cerberus bounded around the corner of the kitchen door and leaped up to "kiss" Medusa awake. It did the trick. She was now ready to make his breakfast. Cerberus sat beside her at rapt attention, as if he'd never seen food preparation before. Medusa put three bowls on the countertop and started to fill each equally with unidentifiable chicken parts, rice, carrots, pigs' ears, and anything she could find left over from the previous night's dinner. Cerberus began to slide around the floor. By now six large streams of drool were pouring from the sides of his mouths and it was hard for him to keep a grip on the slimy tiles. Medusa put the bowls down and hastily removed her hands as Cerberus's greedy heads plowed in, each racing to see which one could finish first and start on one of the others. Medusa got the drool mop out, cleaned up the mess, and then fixed her own breakfast.

When Medusa had got herself washed up and dressed, she pulled down a scarf from the coat stand, put Cerberus's leashes on, and headed for the door. Her mom's disembodied voice called out when she heard the door opening.

"Off to the stump, dear?" she called.

"Yes, Mom," Medusa called back.

"Well," called her mom, "have a nice time, be home for dinner, and don't—"

"Turn anyone to stone, I know. Bye," called Medusa, and closed the door behind her.

Medusa and her friends met at the stump most weekends. It was a huge old tree stump, which stood on a grassy mound with a splendid view of Athens below it. They had tried many times to count the rings to work out how old the tree had been, but they never managed. Let's just say it was old. Medusa and Cerberus puffed up the hill, then Cerberus caught sight of Chiron at the stump and ran ahead to greet him.

"Get this mutt off me." Chiron grimaced as Medusa approached. Cerberus was darting around Chiron's legs and had now jumped up and was swinging from his tail. Chiron was a centaur. He had the torso of a boy and the body of a horse—well, a foal. Chiron swung around in circles trying to grab the puppy but he couldn't reach his own tail.

"Less of that, you." Medusa smiled and pulled Cerberus off.

"I wish he wouldn't do that," said Chiron, flicking his tail to get the drool off.

"Well," giggled Medusa, "if you have a dog toy hanging off your butt, what do you expect?"

"Not too cold for you today?" Chiron grinned. "Wouldn't benefit from a hat?"

"Oh, don't even start," Medusa huffed.

"What was that all about?" laughed Chiron.

"Oh, you know, the Chumpions." Medusa sighed.

"Come on, Med." Chiron smiled as he leaned down and patted her shoulder. "You know they're idiots. Just don't listen to them. They call me 'specky four legs' every day but I don't care." Chiron adjusted his glasses.

"That's actually quite clever for them," said Medusa. "They must have sat up late using their brain cell to come up with that one. How come they're so popular—that's what I want to know."

"They're the Champions and we're the Freaks, and that's all that matters to anyone," said Chiron, smiling halfheartedly.

They sat and looked out over Athens. Plumes of smoke curled up over the city from the bakeries and blacksmiths, and they could hear tradesmen advertising their wares to the Saturday morning crowds.

"Speaking of freaks . . ." Chiron grinned.

They watched as a little pair of horns came into view heading up the hill toward them.

The horns became a bull and the bull became a boy. It was Mino, the Minotaur. He had the body of a boy and the head of a bull. As Mino puffed up the hill, Cerberus ran down to accompany him.

"You're getting earlier, Mino," called Medusa.

"I know," Mino wheezed as he approached. "It's starting to make more sense now."

Mino had been late ever since his dad started building. When Mino was born, his dad decided a nursery was necessary. Then a playroom. Then an extra den. He hired some contractors, who had stayed for two years building room after room, corridor after corridor, until everyone forgot what the original plan had been. As a result, it took Mino and his family about an hour to find their way from the den to the kitchen. It took two painful hours to get to a bathroom from anywhere and a long, long time to find their way to the front door. At one point, Mino hadn't seen his parents for four days. Mino's mom now spent most of her time cleaning and his dad had retreated to one of the bathrooms, where he soaked in very hot baths for days at a time making new plans.

"I took the fourth left instead of the fifth after the study," said Mino. "I think that's where I went wrong. Anyway, how are you guys?"

"Fine," said Medusa and Chiron unconvincingly.

"It's the Chumpions again," Chiron confessed. "They've been bugging Med."

"Oooo, those shiny cretins," huffed Mino. "What I'd give to gore them. Just one of them even, Theseus maybe."

"You can't gore them, Mino." Medusa sighed. "No more than I can turn them to stone."

"Do you think you really could turn them to stone?" asked Chiron. "I've never *actually* seen you do it."

"I don't know." Medusa frowned. "What sort of lame Gorgon am I? My mom does insist though that I turned my pet hamster, Truffles, to stone when I was younger."

Cerberus looked up worriedly.

"A hamster?" asked Mino. "What did Truffles do to deserve that?"

"Oh, I don't know," Medusa said. "I was young—maybe he looked at me funny."

"Remind me not to look at you with my cheeks full," said Chiron.

The friends laughed. They stood up and started down the hill. It was getting toward lunchtime and the pastry shops would be opening soon.

CHAPTER V

MEDUSA AND HER FRIENDS DECIDED THAT THEY needed a united front. When Monday morning came, they met up early and walked to school together. The plan was that it would be harder for the Champions' little brains to insult all of them at once, so arriving at school would be less harrowing. They chatted happily together until they turned the corner and looked up toward the school gates.

There was nobody there.

"I can't see them," said Medusa. "Can you see them, Mino?"

He peered up the road. "Not a sausage," Mino said. "Maybe they're just inside the gates."

The three walked up the road and looked around. Not a soul.

"That's strange," Chiron said. "The Chumpions never give up the opportunity to mock in the morning. Where could they be?"

"I don't know and I don't care," said Mino.

This was far better than usual, but slightly unnerving. The three friends walked up the steps and down the corridor toward their classroom. As they got closer, they could hear the sound of chatter coming from inside. Why would everyone have gone to school early today?

"Oh," said Chiron.

"Oh what?" Medusa asked.

"We forgot," said Chiron. "They announce the class trips today."

Of course, thought Medusa. The class trips, how could she forget? They walked into the room, and Miss Medea turned around and squinted at the new arrivals. Miss Medea was the palest woman in town. She permanently looked as if someone had just told her that her cat had died—tragically.

"Ahhh, finally," said Miss Medea. "I'm so glad you frea—children could join us. Well, hurry up and sit down with the rest of your group."

The three friends took their seats in front of the Champions. Miss Medea had thought that placing Medusa and her friends in Group A with the Champions was a hoot. Medusa considered it an act of purest evil. The children of Group B smiled gleefully while the Champions stared at the three friends as if they were something found on the bottom of sandals.

"It's good that you three don't care as much about the class trips as the rest of us," continued Miss Medea, cleaning out the underside of a nail with her pocketknife. "It means that the children who do care have already bagged their trip of choice."

Group B was smiling from ear to ear and whispering

excitedly about their plans. Mino felt something wet thud against the back of his head. He looked around to see Theseus glaring at him, straw in hand.

"Group B," explained Miss Medea, gesturing toward the delighted children with her knife, "were all here at quarter to nine. They have decided that they would prefer the trip to Neptune's Waterworld."

Group B cheered.

"It seems," said Miss Medea, "that Neptune's
Waterworld—"

Group B cheered again.

"—is a very popular attraction."

"Very popular" was an understatement. Every child in town would have sold their granny to go to Neptune's Waterworld. It had opened a month ago and was already booked solid until spring. Nobody could lay their hands on a ticket for love or money.

Medusa put her hand up gingerly.

"Yes, Mendoza?" said Miss Medea, flicking her nail's contents over the children's heads.

"It's Medusa," said Medusa.

"That's what I said." Miss Medea smiled.

"Miss," said Medusa. "Can't we *all* go to Neptune's Waterworld?"

Group B cheered again. Medusa felt a spitball ricochet off one of her headsnakes; they all hissed at Theseus.

"Heavens no!" Miss Medea laughed. "Do you think this school is made of money? Neptune's Waterworld"—a cheer from Group B—"is very popular, you know. We only managed to get six tickets, and those tickets have gone to the group that was interested enough to get here early. Group B."

Group B cheered triumphantly.

"But not to worry, Group A," smiled Miss Medea. "We have a wonderful trip planned for the six of you."

A hush fell over Group A. What could it be? Hades's Underworld wasn't as new as Waterworld, but some of the rides were still pretty good. Or a day at the chariot races was still always fun.

"Nobody goes away empty-handed, Group A," Miss Medea said, relishing the tension. "You lucky children will all be going on an exciting . . . camping trip."

Group A groaned.

Group B cheered.

"Up Mount Olympus!" announced Miss Medea, and the collective groan of Group A was drowned out completely by Group B's huge cheer.

Perseus leaned over Medusa's shoulder. "You and your freaky friends are going to pay for this," he hissed before her headsnakes drove him back.

"Miss," asked Cassandra, "do we have to go with the freaks? They smell."

"I'm afraid so, Cassy." Miss Medea smiled again, starting on another nail. "It'll be character-building."

"They don't have a character to build on," Chiron moaned.

"That's enough of that sort of talk, Chiffon," said Miss Medea. "The three of you would do well to take a leaf out of the Champions' book."

"They don't have any books," Mino said. "They can't read."

At this point Group A erupted in a bout of

name-calling until Miss Medea screamed, "SHUT UP!" and threw her pocketknife over their heads with terrific force, so it landed with a *twang* in the window frame behind them. The children shut up.

"Now," said Miss Medea, "bright and early next Saturday morning the bus will be outside the school. It will take Group A to the bottom of Mount Olympus and Group B to Nept"—Miss Medea thought for a second—"to their destination."

61

Group B cheered anyway. "Mr. Argonaut and I will be there to wave you off."

"Won't you be coming with us, miss?" asked Medusa.

"Goodness no," Miss Medea said. "Saturday's my poker night."

Medusa could hear Theseus's knuckles crunching behind her.

CHAPTER VI

"**I'**M NOT GOING," SAID MEDUSA.

"It's not open to debate," said Medusa's mom.

It was Friday evening, and Medusa was sitting in the garden watching her mom rake up the leaves that gathered around the feet of the petrified postmen. Cerberus was snuffling around at the bottom of the fence. He had spotted a squirrel a second ago but it had darted away, and now his heads were in disagreement as to which direction it had gone.

Medusa and her friends had just had the worst week of their lives and they were not looking forward to the weekend. The Champions blamed them entirely for not bagging the trip to Neptune's Waterworld and had made all of their lives a living Hades.

On Tuesday after school, Theseus pushed Mino into a door so hard that it had taken them more than an hour to get his horns unstuck. On Thursday the Champions took turns following Chiron around all day with a shovel and bucket "in case he needed to go." And today Perseus had thrown a terrified mouse onto Medusa's head and she'd had to battle with her own hair to save it.

64

"I'm ill," said Medusa, and gave a small, unconvincing cough.

"No you're not," said Medusa's mom. She pushed the last of the leaves down into a basket and came over to sit next to Medusa. "It might not be so bad. All your friends are going."

"It *will* be so bad," Medusa groaned. "I can see my friends any weekend and it's much better without those idiots there."

"Well, you'll just have to be brave, then," said Medusa's mom and stroked one of her headsnakes, which curled around her finger affectionately. "Sometimes you have to face people when you don't want to."

"I don't remember you ever facing someone you didn't want to," Medusa huffed.

"You weren't very big when I had to go to the Central Post Office, dear," said Medusa's mom. "That was the last place on earth I wanted to go. Can you imagine how embarrassing it was to apologize for all these poor petrified postmen?"

"That's not even easy to say." Medusa smiled.

"It certainly isn't." Her mom smiled back. "I had to go down there and face all those irate postmen who thought that all Gorgons were monsters. I really didn't want to do it."

"Then why did you?" Medusa asked.

"Well, because I didn't want the life for you that Gran has had. Plus, I was sick of collecting our mail, and your dad put his back out lugging these through to the garden." She pointed at the postmen.

"I'm missing the message here." Medusa grinned.

"Well, I'm not sure there is one," Medusa's mom confessed. "But I do know I felt better for doing it.

Why don't you take Cerberus with you? He'll sort out those Chumpions."

"I don't think I'd be allowed to take Cerb," Medusa said.

"We'll think of something," said Medusa's mom.

Cerberus heard his name being mentioned and came running over in case it involved biscuits. Medusa ruffled his ears.

"Can we burn the leaves, Mom?" asked Medusa.

"Of course," her mom said. "The posties look pretty in the firelight."

CHAPTER VII

"**...E**IGHT, NINE, TEN, ELEVEN," COUNTED MISS Medea. "Where's twelve? I'm missing a child. Who's missing?" She scanned the squirming children on the bus.

"Miss Medea, Medusa Jones is missing, miss," Perseus called from the back.

"She's holding everyone up, miss," Cassandra complained. "Perhaps we had better go without her, miss."

Mino looked around and scowled at Cassandra. He wondered where Medusa was, but was pleased that he wasn't the last to arrive for once.

"We can't go without her, miss," Chiron called. "I spoke to her last night, and she is coming."

"She'll be busy doing her hair," tittered Cassandra, and the Champions all giggled.

Miss Medea tapped her toe on the ground and looked at her sundial. It was quarter past already. "Well," she said, "one selfish little frea—girl can't hold everyone else up. The gates of Neptune's Waterworld"—Group B cheered—"have already opened so you'll just have to go without—"

"There she is," Chiron shouted. Everyone peered in the direction he was pointing. There was Medusa struggling up the road with a backpack and a large carpetbag, which she was slowly heaving behind her. Miss Medea got off the bus and waited for Medusa to arrive.

"You are late, Miss Jones." Miss Medea glared.

"I know, miss," Medusa wheezed. "I'm sorry. My bags are heavy." She took off her backpack and tried to get her breath back.

"Have you ever heard of economical packing, Madeira?" asked Miss Medea. "What on earth have you got there? You're only going away for a night, not a week."

"I'm sorry, miss," Medusa said. Her bag started to move toward the bus but she stopped it with her foot.

"When I travel, Medulla," continued Miss Medea, "I carry only a fresh pair of underwear and my pocketknife. That is quite satisfactory."

Medusa tried hard to get that unpleasant image out of her head.

"Well, get all that junk on board," snapped Miss Medea. "I have to get home and back to bed. Hurry up, hurry up child."

Medusa picked up her backpack and while she pulled it onto her shoulders, Miss Medea grabbed the carpetbag.

"I'll get that!" said Medusa, reaching for the bag, but Miss Medea swung it athletically into the bus as if it weighed nothing. It landed with a thud and what sounded like a whimper.

"What was that?" asked Miss Medea, her eyes narrowing. She started toward the carpetbag that was slowly moving toward Chiron's hooves.

Medusa jumped up onto the bus and lightly whined. "I just hate to see antique bags treated like that, miss. My father gave that bag to me. His father gave it to him and his father gave it to him and his—"

"Yes, yes, yes," interrupted Miss Medea, stepping back off the bus. "Just get your junk on board and let's get this freak show going to Neptune's Waterworld."

Group B cheered.

"SHUT UP!" screamed Miss Medea; enough of her weekend had already been wasted. Group B shut up. "Right, children, don't get drowned, lost, or mutilated. Don't disgrace the school and if you do, don't mention my name. I'll see you all on Monday morning for the geometry test. Enjoy!"

With that, Miss Medea slammed the door and banged on the side of the bus. The driver, who had been dozing until this point, suddenly woke up and snapped his whip. The four hefty-looking horses yoked to the bus also woke up and slowly started off down the road. Mino looked out the window and saw that Miss Medea had already gone. He got up to help Medusa with her bags.

"What have you got in here, Med?" he whispered.

"A secret weapon," said Medusa with a wink.

CHAPTER VIII

GROUP A WATCHED IN DISMAY AS GROUP B JUMPED off the bus screaming with joy and ran through the fabulous gates of Neptune's Waterworld. The bus moved off and the remaining children peered out of the back until the theme park was just a wonderfully exciting-looking speck on the horizon.

"Next stop, Mount Olympus!" called the driver cheerily, but nobody cheered back.

The bus rolled on through the busy streets of Athens and then past the quiet suburbs. The last of the houses petered out and soon it was only the occasional farm on the road to Mount Olympus. The cobbled streets ran out too, and then the children were being jiggled about uncomfortably on the rough country roads. Medusa hoped that the Champions weren't going to moan about it the whole way. The children gazed at the passing farms and it seemed to them that even the sheep were wondering why anyone would want to spend a weekend out here.

Gradually the road started to climb higher and higher. Medusa watched the huge horses slow down and soon their breath began to show in the air as they puffed up the slope. She wondered how she would cope with a hill that a horse had trouble getting up. Finally the bus turned a bend and there, towering before them, was Mount Olympus itself— well, most of it. All they could see was about a third of the great mountain; the rest was shrouded in a deep mist.

"Good grief," whispered Chiron. "It's *huge.*"

"So's your big horse's bum. HUR HUR HUR," called a familiar voice from the back of the bus. Chiron chose to ignore it.

Finally the bus pulled up at the base of the mountain track.

"Mount Olympus!" called the driver as if they didn't know. "Everybody off!"

The children reluctantly collected their bags and got off the bus.

"Well," called the driver cheerily, "I'll meet you here at lunchtime tomorrow. You all have a good time now. Good-bye, kids." With that, he closed the bus door and the horses started to move off. Then suddenly they stopped and the driver looked back.

"Watch out for the wolves now!" he called, and gave the children a wink as the bus started off again for Athens.

"Wolves?" said Cassandra. "Miss Medea didn't say anything about wolves."

"I think he was just kidding us," Medusa said, trying to smile along with the "joke."

"Did she ask what you think, viper face?" snapped Perseus.

"Ooo, I'd like to . . ." started Mino, moving toward him, but Chiron grabbed his arm and pulled him back.

"Back off, bull boy," Perseus sneered.

"Yeah . . . horn head." Theseus smiled at his own ingenuity.

"We wouldn't even be in this hole if it weren't for you," Cassandra said. "Once we get to the top of this wretched hill, we might just push you freaks off."

The Champions started to move toward Medusa and her friends. Medusa squatted down and hurriedly opened up her carpetbag.

Cerberus slowly emerged, a bit dazed, one head at a time. "You brought three dogs with you?" asked Theseus, his brow furrowed.

"Good grief!" Perseus gasped as Cerberus wobbled out of the bag. "I thought I'd seen it all. You people just get freakier by the day."

Cerberus had adjusted himself to the light and had now set his six eyes on the Champions. He started to growl. The Champions backed away.

"Get that thing away from us," Cassandra whimpered.

"Why don't you pet him?" Medusa smiled. Cerberus bared three large sets of teeth at the Champions. Mino bent down and gave him a cuddle. Within moments, the Champions had got their packs on and were moving quickly up the hill.

"Who's a good boy?" laughed Mino, petting Cerberus and getting a face full of drool for his trouble.

"I'm glad you thought to bring him," Chiron said.

"It was Mom's idea," said Medusa.

With the Champions well ahead of them, the
three got their packs on and started the long climb up
Mount Olympus.

CHAPTER IX

"**W**HAT A LOVELY VIEW," PUFFED MINO. "LET'S stop and admire it."

"You said that ten minutes ago," said Chiron.

"And ten minutes before that too," said Medusa.

Mino stopped anyway and collapsed with a thud on a large rock.

"Look," he wheezed. "I'm not used to this sort of thing. We don't all have four legs, you know."

"This isn't easy for me either," Chiron snapped. "You should try wobbling up this terrain on hooves."

"Stop squabbling, you two," Medusa said. She put her pack down and got out Cerberus's water bowl. She hadn't had enough room to pack three bowls, so his thirsty heads just had to fight over one.

"Good idea," said Chiron, and got out his canteen.

He gulped down some water and then looked out at the view.

"You are right though, Mino," said Chiron. "It is amazing."

Greece spread out before them. The late afternoon sun had given everything a warm orangey-pink

glow. They could see little farms littered across the landscape like toys. Olive groves were the size of broccoli, and herds of sheep and goats looked like ants from so far up. Far in the distance was Athens, barely recognizable for the huge city that it was. To the east lay the glittering Aegean Sea, on which they could just pick out the billowing white sails of fishing boats. Chiron even fancied that he could see Turkey beyond the Aegean, but they just had to take his word for that.

"I'll bet the Chumpions aren't appreciating this," Medusa said.

"I'm sure they'll only be admiring themselves as usual," said Chiron.

"How far ahead do you think they are anyway?" Medusa asked.

"Who cares?" Mino said. "As long as they're not bothering us."

It had been a good idea to bring Cerberus. Once the Champions laid eyes on him, they had decided it might be best not to bother Medusa and her friends. As the day progressed, Medusa had occasionally caught a glimpse of the three dazzling children bounding effortlessly ahead. Once or twice there had been a little rockfall from above that may have been accompanied by some laughter, but Medusa couldn't be sure.

As Medusa and her friends got higher, the climb got harder. The track became less defined and there were more sheer areas where the children had to scramble up on all fours. Chiron was having a particularly hard time but the friends always managed to help him, even if it did mean getting his tail in their faces now and then.

The sun slipped below the horizon and it was getting colder. Chiron didn't feel the chill too badly, but the others pulled out the shawls that their parents had packed for them.

"I could eat," Mino said.

"What's new?" said Chiron.

Mino scowled at him.

"Maybe we should set up camp and have some dinner," Medusa suggested. "I don't like the look of those clouds up there."

The top of the mountain was shrouded in blue-and-purple clouds, which didn't look as though they were going to clear that night.

"You're right," said Chiron. "So what have we got?"

They looked at one another.

"I couldn't find the kitchen," Mino said. "I was in there last Thursday, but I couldn't remember how I did it."

"That's okay, Mino," said Medusa. "It's not your fault. What about you, Chiron?"

"Well, you know my folks have that thing for raw vegetables," Chiron said. "I doubt you'd really want to share my dinner."

"Or share a tent with you afterward." Mino smiled. "What about you, Med? Your mom's a good cook. What did you bring?"

Medusa grinned; she'd watched her mom preparing her food and it looked great. "She made me lots of moussaka, with lamb and rice, and a huge bag of olives."

"Oh boy!" Mino said, salivating. "Your mom's moussaka is to kill for. Where is it all?"

"I packed it in the carpetbag," Medusa said, "with . . ."

The three looked around at Cerberus.

Cerb gave a soft and slightly meaty burp.

The three sat, suddenly very aware of their rumbling stomachs.

"I'll bet the Chumpions have brought the food of the gods," sighed Medusa.

"They wouldn't share even if we were starving," said Mino.

"We could ask," Chiron said. "What's the harm?"

They thought for a moment. None of them really wanted to ask the Champions for anything, but their stomachs were saying otherwise.

"Chiron's right," Medusa said eventually. "We might as well."

They got their packs on and started upward to look for the Champions.

It took a while, but eventually Medusa spotted a flame in the distance. As they got closer they could hear the Champions laughing, probably about the misfortunes of others. The Champions were sitting in

a clearing; they had a little campfire going and a rabbit slowly cooking on a spit above it. They looked over when they heard Chiron's hooves approaching.

"Look who it is," Perseus laughed, "horseboy and the mutant mountaineers."

They all laughed.

"What's a mutant?" asked Theseus, but they ignored him.

"We thought you'd fallen off the mountain hours ago," Cassandra said.

"Pity," said Perseus.

"What's the point in this?" Mino asked Medusa. "I'd rather eat my own leg than dine with these idiots."

Medusa agreed, but sighed and gave it a try anyway.

"We thought you might like to eat with us," she said, trying to crack a smile at the Champions.

The Champions burst out laughing. They laughed and laughed and finally when Perseus could breathe properly again, he gasped, "Us? Eat . . . with you? We are the Champions. We do not feast with freaks. We dine with kings and queens, emperors and emperoresses, dukes and . . ."

"Dukesses?" tried Theseus.

"The very idea!" Cassandra guffawed.

"The nerve!" tittered Perseus.

"The dog," said Chiron.

"What?" said Perseus.

"Look behind you." Medusa smiled.

The Champions looked over at Cerberus, who had managed, with the aid of his three heads, to pull the rabbit off the spit and was hungrily waiting for it to cool down.

"Your Freaky Fido has ruined our starter," spat Perseus at Medusa.

"Serves you right," Medusa spat back.

"Come, Champions," said Perseus, gathering up his expensive backpack. "Onward and upward, away from these . . . creatures."

The rest of the Champions picked up their stuff, tutting, and started off.

"Perseus," said Cassandra, "it's awful cloudy up ahead."

"We do not camp with carnies, Cassandra," Perseus snapped, and strode off up the path, the Champions following behind.

"Bye," Medusa called.

"See ya," called Chiron.

"Wouldn't want t'be ya," called Mino.

They walked over to the fire and Medusa took the rabbit from Cerberus, who looked disappointed.

"You have had plenty already." She smiled, stroking his ears.

"That all worked out rather well," Chiron said, producing his vegetables from his pack. "Rabbit stew, anyone?"

"Let's set up camp," Medusa said. "I'm not going any farther tonight."

CHAPTER X

"**M**ED . . . MED . . . WAKE UP, MED. WAKE UP." Chiron was pushing Medusa's shoulder as if he wanted her to wake up but didn't want to disturb her.

"Monkey," murmured Medusa. "Bicycle. Sorry . . . so sorry." She rolled over.

Chiron poked her hard in the neck. *"Med!"*

Medusa woke with a start. She sat up in her sleeping bag and tried to focus. It was pitch-black in the tent, apart from the dim light cast by Chiron's oil lamp.

"What time is it?" Medusa grumbled, rubbing her eyes.

"How many sundials have you seen that work at night?" asked Chiron. "I don't know what time it is. Maybe about three A.M."

"Chiron," Medusa said, "with the storm, the rock I'm lying on, and your farts, I only managed to drop off an hour ago. You better have a good reason to have woken me."

"Listen," Chiron said.

"To what?" Medusa frowned.

"Just listen," Chiron insisted.

Medusa listened. She heard the noise that had kept her awake for the past four hours. By the time they had managed to erect their flimsy tent, the storm had set in. The wind wailed and howled and beat the canvas as if it were desperate to get at them.

"I hear the storm, Chiron," Medusa huffed.

"I hear something else," whispered Chiron. "Listen more closely."

"If you're trying to spook me," said Medusa, "I won't be—" She stopped mid-sentence.

She heard it. It was faint, hidden by the noise of the wind and rain, but she heard it.

It sounded like screaming.

"It sounds like screaming," Medusa whispered, her eyes growing wider. Now that she could hear it, she wondered how she had missed it in the first place. And yet now that she could hear it, she wished that she couldn't.

It was a horrible sound and she wished it would go away.

"What do you think it is?" whispered Medusa.

"Maybe the bus driver wasn't joking," Chiron said. "Maybe there are wolves up here."

"I don't think so," said Medusa. "There are no wolves up here. What would they eat?"

"Campers," Chiron said.

Medusa ignored that thought. "Anyway, wolves howl. That's not a howl. That's a scream."

"Well, if it's not us," Chiron said, "and it's not the wolves, there's only one other solution."

Medusa swiveled around and flicked one of Mino's

ears. Mino had dropped off first and was snoring like a fully grown bull. Medusa felt some satisfaction in flicking him.

Mino woke with a jolt.

"Huh? Who? I'll gore ya. . . ." he blurted, and looked around.

"Mino," said Medusa, "we hear screaming."

"You'll hear more screaming if you flick my ear again," Mino said.

"We think it's the Champions," said Chiron.

"Let 'em scream," said Mino, and turned back over in his sleeping bag.

Medusa flicked his other ear. Mino shot back up.
"If anyone else had done that . . ." Mino growled,
glaring at Medusa. Then he heard the screams.
He shut up.

"What'll we do?" Chiron asked.
"We have to go look," said Medusa. She
amazed herself even as she said it.

"Why?" Mino asked. "They wouldn't
cross the road to help us."

"I know," Medusa answered.
"But we're not them,
and we can't just sit
here and listen
to that. It's
awful."

It was awful and it had grown more desperate too.

"Even if we did try to find them," Chiron said, "how can we? It's as black as Hades out there."

"Good point," Mino said. "Well, good night, then."

"Cerb," said Medusa.

"What about him?" Mino asked.

"He's got three noses," Medusa said. "He could find a flea in this storm."

Cerberus looked around at the sound of his name. He had been sitting at the door of the tent listening to the screams for the past hour, wondering why nobody seemed bothered.

The three friends got out of their sleeping bags. They were already dressed, thanks to the cold, but they pulled on their leather shawls to protect themselves against the rain and headed out into the darkness.

CHAPTER XI

"**S**LOW DOWN, CERB!" MEDUSA SHOUTED.

Cerberus may only have been a puppy but he was pulling his leashes with the strength of an ox. Medusa, Chiron, and Mino could hardly see a thing except for when the lightning would suddenly illuminate the steep craggy rock face, which Cerberus was hurriedly pulling them up.

The wind bit hard into their faces, and Chiron found it even tougher to get purchase on the wet rocks in the darkness.

"This is nuts," Mino yelled. "We're going to fall off and then there'll be two sets of screams."

"I don't think they're far now," Medusa shouted back. "The screams are getting louder. Cerb is definitely on their trail."

She wiped the rain out of her eyes and quickly got her grip back on the leashes in case they slipped out of her hands. If she lost Cerberus she didn't like to imagine what they would do.

They climbed in the darkness until at last Chiron spotted something in one of the lightning flashes.

"There!" he yelled. "I think I see them."

They looked in the direction Chiron was pointing, and at the next flash they all saw the Champions. Three figures huddled together on a ledge. There seemed to be no path connecting them to the mountain. How on earth did they get there?

As the friends got closer, they could pick out the three terrified faces of the Champions. Medusa had only ever seen that expression before on her garden ornaments, and it was far more disturbing in the flesh. The three friends shuffled along the path until it stopped. There was a gaping chasm between them and the Champions. They peered down into it but couldn't see the bottom; the rock slipped away into the endless dark.

At last Perseus looked up out of the whimpering huddle and spotted them. Medusa had never seen a look of relief on his irritatingly handsome face before.

"Help me!" Perseus shouted.

Cassandra and Theseus looked up and saw Medusa and her friends.

"Help us!" shouted Cassandra, and frowned at Perseus.

"We're too young and pretty to die," Perseus sobbed.

"What happened?" shouted Medusa.

"There was a rockfall!" Cassandra screamed.

"Rocks come down," shouted Theseus, "path go away."

"Always a man of words," Mino muttered.

"Never mind what happened," Perseus wailed. "Just help us, for the love of Zeus!"

The wind howled around the three terrified

Champions. Half of their camp had fallen down the gorge, and the other half flapped violently around them in shreds.

The friends huddled together to talk over the wind.

"What can we do?" asked Chiron.

"Leave 'em," Mino said.

"As tempting as that sounds, Mino," said Medusa, "we can't just leave them. We have to at least try."

"Rope," Chiron said.

"We don't have any rope," said Mino.

"I know we don't have any rope," Chiron said. "But maybe the Chumpions do."

"Good idea," said Medusa. She turned to the Champions.

"Do you have any rope?" Medusa called.

"Rope fall down hole," shouted Theseus.

"Oh, well," said Mino. "Rope fall down hole. At least we tried. Let's go home."

"Don't leave us!" wailed Perseus.

Cassandra was just chanting now, over and over, "We're gonna die, we're gonna die, we're gonna die, we're gonna die. . . ."

It was the most pitiful thing Medusa had ever heard.

"There must be another way," she said to the others. "Think."

They thought.

Medusa looked around. There wasn't much to work with. Some shrubs, boulders, an old goat skull, and a small tree, which Cerberus was lifting his leg against.

Medusa's eyes twinkled. She had an idea.

"Mino," said Medusa, "see that tree over there?"

Mino looked over. "What about it?" he asked.

"Do you think you could push it over?"

"For you, Med," Mino said with a smile, "I'd fell a forest."

"A bridge!" Chiron grinned, wiping the rain off his glasses. "Why didn't I think of that?"

"Because I'm the beauty *and* the brains of this out-fit." Medusa smiled. She turned to the Champions.

"Stand back!" she shouted.

Perseus looked at the chasm behind him.

"There is no back," he wailed.

"Then stand aside," shouted Medusa. "We're sending over a bridge."

"We're all gonna die, we're all gonna die, we're all gonna die," chanted Cassandra.

Mino squared up to the tree. He'd felled some trees before but this was pretty big for a small Minotaur like him.

"You can do it, Mino," Chiron said.

Mino squatted down like a runner preparing to sprint. He counted to three under his breath and then launched himself at the tree. His horns dug deep into the wood and there was a loud creak as the tree began to uproot.

"Push, Mino, push!" Medusa shouted.

"I . . . . . . AM . . . . . . PUSHING!" grunted Mino.

Stones and dirt flew into the wind as one by one, the roots were pulled up and the tree began to fall.

Cerberus ran about the base of the tree barking furiously. What was the point of peeing on something when someone just comes along and knocks it over?

With an eerie groan, the tree fell and crashed at the feet of the Champions. Chiron and Medusa ran over and helped Mino pull his horns out of the wood.

"Well done! You've saved them." Medusa gave Mino a peck on the cheek.

"I didn't do it for them," Mino said, blushing.

Medusa turned to the Champions. "There's your bridge!" she called. "Come on!" The Champions didn't budge. Their similarity to the postmen was complete: Not only did the Champions share their look of terror but they were now literally scared stiff.

"Move yourselves!" yelled Mino.

But the Champions didn't move.

"They're petrified," said Medusa.

The Champions looked at the tree as they would look at a man-eating tiger.

They weren't going anywhere.

"I'll go," Chiron said.

"Go where?" asked Mino.

"I'll carry them across," Chiron said.

"Your hooves can't handle wet bark, Chiron," Medusa said.

"I've come this far, haven't I?" Chiron smiled. "Anyway, what other option do we have?"

"You're the bravest centaur on the mountain," Medusa said.

"I'm the *only* centaur on the mountain," said Chiron with a frown.

"Good luck, you idiot," Mino said, and patted Chiron's flank.

Chiron clambered up onto the roots of the tree and started to inch his way across. His hooves slid around the bark as if he were straddling a giant icicle. Medusa could barely watch as Chiron slowly began to move forward, jamming his hooves into the bases of branches where he could, trying not to look down into the dark, bottomless chasm. He was about halfway over when one of the branch footholds gave way with a crack and disappeared down into the gloom. Chiron swung his arms wide and managed to grab on to the tree. He looked down into the darkness and shuddered. Medusa and Mino shouted words of

encouragement, and the Champions stared in horror. Chiron pulled himself back to his feet, and bit by bit worked his way along until finally his hooves found the rocky ledge where the Champions were shivering in despair.

"Okay," said Chiron once he had got his breath back. "Who's first?"

"Me!" Perseus shouted and pushed himself forward.

"No, me!" Theseus yelled and grabbed Perseus's cloak to hold him back.

"Ladies first," wailed Cassandra, and joined the scuffle.

"I'm not being left behind," shouted Perseus. "I'm the son of Zeus."

"Oh, Zeus Schmeus," Cassandra spat.

"Anyone on the horse before me gets a fat lip," Theseus growled, and crunched his knuckles.

Perseus turned to Chiron. "We all go," he said.

"All of you? At once?" asked Chiron. "I'm not sure I can . . ."

"Oh, pleeease. Don't leave me here to die," wailed Cassandra, trying to bat her massive eyelashes attractively.

Chiron looked at the tree. It seemed crazy, but the thought of one treacherous crossing compared to another five was very tempting.

"All right," he said. "Get up . . . gently."

The Champions pulled themselves up one by one

and grabbed on tightly to anything they could. Chiron had never been ridden before and this was not a good introduction.

Medusa and Mino watched the pantomime from the other side of the gorge.

"What on earth are they doing?" Mino asked.

"Let's just pray that Chiron knows what he's up to," Medusa whispered.

Chiron started to move toward the tree. With the Champions on board, his hooves felt like lead and it was a struggle to take even one step. It required all his strength to climb onto the trunk and start gingerly toward the gorge. The added weight seemed to help his hooves dig into the bark more solidly, but the grip was still as slippery and now the wind seemed to be howling even more fiercely. Perseus sat on Chiron's back and was gripping tightly around his neck. Cassandra was chanting in the middle,

wrapped around Perseus. At the back was Theseus, with a firm hold on Chiron's tail and facing the wrong way. When the bottomless chasm came into view below, Perseus's grip grew tighter around Chiron's neck. It was all Chiron could do to keep breathing. He slapped Perseus's arm until his grip slightly loosened. Chiron wiped his glasses and inched forward, wedging his hooves into the branches as he went. The rain lashed down against them, and the wind howled and wailed so nobody heard the first cracking noise.

But everyone heard the second one.

CRACK.

The bark began to splinter.

CRACK.

The Champions began to scream.

CRAACK.

The tree began to lurch.

CRAAACKK.

Chiron could feel the wood start to move beneath him.

"It's going to split!" shouted Mino. "It can't take their weight!"

CRAAAACCKKK.

"Run, Chiron! Run!" shouted Medusa.

"I can't!" Chiron yelled.

CRRRAAAACCCKKK.

"We're all going to die!" Cassandra wailed.

"Not if I can help it," said Medusa.

"What?" shouted Mino. He looked around at her. He looked at her eyes.

Medusa's pupils were starting to glow.

The centers glowed orange like the sun but the edges were a ghostly green. The light started to illuminate her cheeks, her nose, her lips. Medusa felt a pain in her temples. A cold pain.

A cold white pain like nothing she had ever felt before. She heard noise, building, building, the sound of a million volcanoes erupting in her head. The wailing of the storm had gone and all she could hear was the sound of the pain growing and growing, cold and white and sweet until suddenly . . . it stopped.

Mino watched as the colors in Medusa's eyes disappeared and were replaced with the purest white he had ever seen.

It lasted for one beautiful second and was gone.

Medusa collapsed. Mino ran to her and held her. She breathed quietly in his arms.

The storm had ended. Chiron looked down.

He had never seen a tree made of stone before.

CHAPTER XII

THE BUS DRIVER HAD ALMOST GIVEN UP ON THEM when the six campers finally appeared, bedraggled and sore, stumbling down the mountainside. Medusa's story was bizarre but when the Champions begrudgingly confirmed the heroics of the night before, the driver forgave them their lateness and set off quickly for home.

All the way back to Athens, the friends laughed and chatted about their adventure. The Champions sat huddled in blankets at the back of the bus, warm now but still shaking from their ordeal.

It was late by the time the bus rolled back into town. The citizens were out for their evening strolls and some waved at the Champions on the bus, but the Champions were too weak to wave back. The bus pulled up at the school and the driver hastily helped the children unload their luggage.

"What's the hurry?" asked Medusa, who wasn't looking forward to the walk home.

"I gotta go tell your story, of course." The bus driver beamed. "How many decent tales do you think a bus driver gets to spread?"

The driver hurriedly led his horses to their stable and then ran off down the street.

"I hope my parents don't hear the story before I get to tell them," Mino said. "I probably won't find them for a couple of days."

"I'm sure they won't," said Medusa.

The six children picked up their bags and started the slow walk home.

The Champions limped behind like wounded animals. Cassandra was still muttering to herself, and

Theseus and Perseus hadn't stopped shaking since they got off Chiron's back.

As they walked down the main street, Medusa started to notice something strange. Was it her imagination or were people staring at them? Medusa and her friends were used to the suspicious gazes of strangers but this was somehow different. People were stopping to look at them and they were smiling. And this wasn't a "look at that hair" smile either, it was something else. Chiron and Mino had noticed it too. It was slightly disconcerting, so the children kept walking. People were pointing now, and someone clapped. Then someone else clapped, and slowly the clapping became applause. Medusa and her friends stopped and looked with bewilderment at all the happy faces. People were cheering now.

"Hurrah!" shouted a bald man none of them knew.

"Well done!" another stranger yelled.

A crowd had formed in the street and everyone was clapping and cheering Medusa and her friends.

"Hurrah for the Champions!" shouted a woman with a baby.

Perseus looked up.

"Hurrah for the *new* Champions!" the crowd called.

Medusa couldn't believe what she was hearing.

"New Champions?" Perseus muttered. "New Champions?"

"But *we're* the Champions," Theseus said, somewhat confused.

"Yes," said Cassandra, who had stopped her gibbering, "we're the Champions around here."

The applause and cheering washed over Medusa, Chiron, and Minos like a warm breeze. They had never been popular before. It felt quite nice.

Then Medusa heard a different voice.

"They're not Champions." It was Perseus.

"We didn't need their help," Theseus called.

"We're the Champions; we managed fine without them!" Cassandra yelled.

"How can *they* be Champions?" shouted Perseus.

"They're just a bunch of freaks!"

The crowd went silent.

Medusa felt her headsnakes quiver.

"Well, nobody's perfect,"
said Medusa.

This book was art directed and designed by Marijka Kostiw. It was edited by Rachel Griffiths and Arthur A. Levine. The jacket art was created using pencil, watercolor, and acrylic paints. The interior art was created with pencil. The text was set in 14 point Adobe Garamond Pro regular, a typeface based on the type designs of sixteenth-century printer Claude Garamond. The title type was hand-lettered in part by Ross Collins, and set in Chauncy Deluxxe Medium. The display font is Lithos Pro, which was designed for Adobe by Carol Twombly; the Lithos font family is based on the lettering from ancient Greek inscriptions. The book was typeset by Marijka Kostiw, and the production was supervised by Susan Jeffers Casel. The book was printed and bound at Quebecor. Manufacturing was supervised by Jess White.